THE CREEPY CLASSICS

CHILDREN'S COLLECTION

Dados Internacionais de Catalogação na Publicação (CIP) de acordo com ISBD

S874d Stoker, Bram.
Dracula / Bram Stoker. - Jandira, SP : W. Books, 2025
128 p. ; 12,80cm x 19,80 cm - (Classics).

ISBN: 978-65-5294-188-6

1. Literatura inglesa. 2. Terror. 3. Clássicos. 4. Fantasia. 5. Imaginação.
6. Suspense. I. Título. II. Série.

2025-2536 CDD 823.91
CDU 821.111-3

Elaborada por Lucio Feitosa - CRB-8/8803
Índice para catálogo sistemático:
1. Literatura inglesa 823.91
2. Literatura inglesa 821.111-3

The Creepy Classics Collection

Text based on the original story by Bram Stoker,
adapted by Gemma Barder
Illustrations by Nick Moffatt

1st edition in 2025
www.cirandacultural.com.br

DRACULA

BRAM STOKER

W. Books

Count Dracula

A mysterious Romanian nobleman

Jonathan Harker

A young solicitor

Mina Murray

Jonathan's fiancée

LUCY WESTENRA

Mina's best friend

ARTHUR HOLMWOOD

Lucy's fiancé

DR SEWARD

A doctor

ABRAHAM VAN HELSING

Dr Seward's friend

Chapter One

Jonathan Harker stared up at the looming towers of Castle Dracula. A cold wind whistled through the grey stone courtyard. The rusted iron gates screeched back and forth.

Jonathan had been given his first big project at the law firm he worked at in London, and he was excited. His job was to travel to Romania

– to a place called Transylvania – to help an old nobleman complete the purchase of a house in England.

It was an easy job. All he had to do was hand over some papers and get them signed, but Jonathan had never travelled to Eastern Europe before and he was enjoying his adventure.

When he arrived in Romania, Jonathan wrote to his fiancée, Mina.

Dearest Mina,

This morning I arrived safely in the country of Romania. It is a beautiful part of the world, and everyone I meet is friendly and helpful. Tomorrow I will travel to Transylvania, to the home of Count Dracula. Our business should not take more than a couple of days, then I will be heading home to plan our wedding!

Jonathan folded the letter and popped it into an envelope. He was exhausted from his travels and keen to climb into bed in the small hotel he was staying in.

'Excuse me,' said Jonathan, politely. 'Could you post this letter for me? I am headed to Transylvania tomorrow.'

The young maid at the counter took the letter, staring at Jonathan with fear in her eyes. 'Did you say … Transylvania?' she asked.

'Yes,' replied Jonathan. 'I have business with a man called Count Dracula, who I believe has a rather impressive castle in the region.'

The maid's hands began to tremble. 'Oh …' she said. 'Oh, you poor man. I have heard terrible tales of the count – things that gave me nightmares for weeks!'

Jonathan smiled. 'I am sure they are just stories,' he said. 'I believe he lives a rather lonely life up there. Thank you for taking my letter. Now I must be heading to bed.'

'Wait!' said the maid, holding her hands up to block Jonathan's path. 'Please, take this.' The maid removed her necklace, which had a small wooden cross attached.

‘That is very kind of you, miss, but I couldn’t possibly,’ said Jonathan, as the maid thrust the necklace into his hands.

‘Please, I beg of you,’ she said. ‘Just keep it in your pocket – and I will pray for you.’

Jonathan forced a smile and placed the cross in his pocket. He had not met many people from Romania, so he did not want to seem impolite. Handing crosses to strangers might be one of their customs.

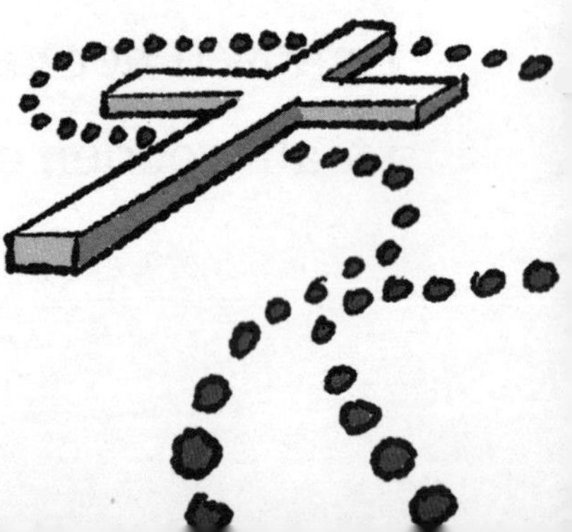

CHAPTER TWO

The following morning, Jonathan was met at the hotel by a carriage sent by Count Dracula himself. Jonathan was impressed by the size of the carriage, which was lined with deep red velvet. He was less impressed by the silent, sullen driver.

Jonathan watched out of the window as the rolling Romanian countryside gave way to dark forests, and the smooth road they

sullen
To be angry or sulky.

were travelling on became rockier.

As night fell and Jonathan was starting to feel like their journey would never end, the carriage came to an abrupt stop. The silent driver opened the door and removed Jonathan's suitcase, before turning the carriage around and departing immediately. Jonathan was left alone, staring up at Castle Dracula. He put his hand in his pocket and felt for the necklace. Then, slowly, he made his way inside.

'Mr Harker?' said a voice that made Jonathan jump. A man had appeared behind him as if from nowhere. He was tall and very thin. His long nose peeked over a long white moustache and he was dressed from head to toe in black.

'Yes,' Jonathan replied. 'Count Dracula?'

The tall man nodded and smiled. 'Indeed. I am very pleased to have you here.'

Jonathan swallowed. He suddenly felt very cold, even though there was a roaring fire in the castle's entrance hall.

'Let me show you to your room,' Count Dracula said, 'then you will eat. You must be hungry after your journey.'

'Yes,' Jonathan said, picking up his suitcase. 'I am a little.'

Jonathan's eyes darted around the castle as they walked. There seemed to be endless corridors and dark staircases, twisting this way and that way.

'My castle can be confusing,' Count Dracula said, as though reading Jonathan's mind. 'This will be your room.' He opened a heavy wooden door to reveal a pleasant-looking room with a large bed and a beautiful view of the countryside from its window. 'Now, let me show you to the dining hall.'

Jonathan tried to keep track of yet more corridors and staircases as he followed the mysterious count through the castle. The dining table was already laid with a magnificent feast, but there was only one plate.

'Excuse me,' said the count, 'but I have already eaten. I will leave you to your meal, but I look forward to knowing you better, Mr Harker. Goodnight.'

With that, the count left the room so silently that Jonathan was not sure if he had really gone. He ate his meal quickly and somehow found his way back to his bedroom.

As Jonathan sat on his bed, he tried to make sense of the strange, unsettling feeling he'd had from the moment he stepped out of the carriage. The castle was dark and unwelcoming. His host was polite but strange. Not unfriendly, but not in any way kind or warm.

Jonathan crossed the room and locked his bedroom door, then he took the cross from his coat pocket and hung it on his bedpost, just above his head.

Exhausted from his travels, Jonathan fell into a restless sleep. He tossed from side to side, dreaming of bats flapping against his window. When he woke the following morning, it felt as though he had not slept at all.

Chapter Three

The daylight that streamed through the castle that morning made Jonathan feel a little better. He was determined to complete the business he had with Count Dracula and start his journey home.

Thinking of Mina and their wedding made him cheerful as he left his room with the papers that needed to be signed under his arm. But as he made his way down the corridors and staircases to where he thought he might find the count, he instead got hopelessly lost. He opened doors to drawing rooms and libraries, breakfast rooms and games rooms. They were all empty and covered with dust – as though no one had used them for months, or even years.

Finally, Jonathan gave up. He somehow found his way back to his bedroom. When he pushed open the heavy door, he found a plate on his dressing table with a sandwich. The count would not be joining him for lunch, it seemed.

***

Jonathan stared out of his window. His room was high up in the castle and he could see miles of beautiful forests and a river that glistened under the setting sun. As darkness fell, Jonathan sensed a presence behind him. 'It's beautiful, isn't it?' said Count Dracula. Jonathan jumped back. He had not heard his bedroom door open. In fact, he was certain he had locked it.

'Y-yes,' he said, startled. 'Your Grace, I have been looking for you all day. Here are the papers you need to sign for your new property in England.'

'Forgive me,' said the count, swooping a hand to gracefully pick up the papers on Jonathan's dressing table. 'I have been … busy. I shall see to these as soon as I can.'

Suddenly, the count stumbled

back. Jonathan held out his arms to steady him. The count was staring at Jonathan's bed, his eyes wide in terror.

'Are you all right, Your Grace?'

The count straightened up and cleared his throat. 'I'm perfectly well,' he said. And with that, he swiftly left the room.

Jonathan was confused. What could have scared the count

in such a way? Then Jonathan noticed the necklace with the wooden cross that was still hanging on his bedpost.

***

That night, Jonathan once again had terrible nightmares. And the following day, once again, the count was nowhere to be seen. Jonathan roamed the corridors until he came to the count's bedroom. He knocked politely, then slowly pushed open the door and stepped inside.

Just like all the other rooms Jonathan had found, the count's bedroom was covered in thick dust. The plush bedcovers had not been slept in, and spiderwebs hung everywhere. To one side there was a doorway that led to a steep spiral staircase. Jonathan followed it downwards. It twisted on and on until the walls felt cold and damp. Finally, he arrived in a dark, windowless basement. The air was freezing and thick with a horrible smell. On the floor was a long, thin box with a rusted brass plate on top. As Jonathan stepped closer, he realised it was not a box at all. It was a coffin! And the name on the plate said: Dracula.

With trembling hands, Jonathan pushed the lid off the coffin. To his horror, he found Count Dracula lying inside, his arms crossed over his chest.

Jonathan's whole body began to tremble with fear. Who – or *what* – was this strange man? Why did he sleep during the day – and in a coffin of all things? Why was he so afraid of the simple cross Jonathan had been given?

Without another thought, Jonathan climbed back up the spiral staircase and returned to his own bedroom. He packed his suitcase and searched for the entrance hall he had arrived through. Although he did not know what Count Dracula was, he knew he must leave Dracula's castle before the sun set.

Chapter Four

Mina Murray and her best friend, Lucy Westenra, were on holiday in the seaside town of Whitby in England. Lucy's aunt had kindly invited the young women to stay, and they were enjoying themselves tremendously.

Their favourite thing to do was to climb the famous 199 steps up to the ruins of Whitby Abbey. They would sit on a bench and catch their breath in the church yard. They liked to exchange spooky stories they had heard.

'My aunt's neighbour told me a lady dressed all in white roams the ruins at night,' said Lucy. 'You can see her looking out of one of the windows where there isn't a floor to stand on!'

Mina laughed. 'That's *nothing*,' she said. 'The old groundskeeper told me that most of the old graves here are empty!'

Lucy placed a hand over her mouth with shock. 'But … why?' she asked, breathlessly.

'Nobody knows,' replied Mina in a hushed voice. The two friends stared at each other for a moment before dissolving into fits of giggles.

'Anyway,' said Mina. 'More importantly, have you made a decision?'

Lucy sighed. 'I have,' she replied. 'I wrote the letters this morning.

I have decided to marry Arthur. I truly love him, Mina.'

Part of the reason why Mina and Lucy had travelled away from London to Whitby was so that Lucy could make up her mind who she was going to marry. She had received two proposals: one from a man called Dr Seward, and one from a man called Arthur Holmwood.

Although Dr Seward was nice, respectable and had a very good job, Lucy knew her heart belonged to Arthur. Arthur was lively and fun

– and he was also the son of a lord.

Mina took her friend's hand and pulled her up from the bench. 'Well then,' she said. 'We had better make our way back into town to post those letters!'

***

When the two friends arrived back at Lucy's aunt's house, they found a letter waiting for Mina.

'Oh!' cried Mina, happily. 'It is Jonathan's handwriting!' She hurriedly opened the letter and smiled.

'He has arrived safely in Romania. Tomorrow he travels to a place called Transylvania. I hope his host, Count Dracula, is friendly!'

CHAPTER FIVE

'My dear girls, have you heard the news?' asked Lucy's aunt a week later. 'There was a terrible shipwreck last night during the storm. The only thing that made it off the ship was a large box that washed up on the shore.'

Lucy and Mina put down their teacups and looked up from the breakfast table.

'How dreadful!' said Lucy.

'What was in the box?' asked Mina.

Lucy's aunt shrugged. 'No one knows. It disappeared before anyone could go and retrieve it. Although some people are saying it was actually a coffin!'

This gave the two friends much to talk about. Then the topic changed to what they would do that day, which was the last day of their holiday. They decided to walk up the 199 steps for one last time.

'I will be sad to leave Whitby,' said Lucy. 'But I can't wait to see Arthur!'

Mina smiled, then sighed heavily. 'I have not heard from Jonathan for a whole week,' she said, gloomily. 'He was only meant to stay in Transylvania a couple of days, then start his journey back to England. I just hope that he is all right.'

***

That night, there was another storm. At midnight, Mina woke to bright flashes of lightning that filled her bedroom, followed by deep, rumbling thunder. She pulled on her dressing gown and tiptoed to Lucy's room to see if her friend was also awake.

As Mina crept inside, she saw that Lucy's bed was empty and her window was wide open. *She must be sleepwalking again*, thought Mina, remembering how her friend used to sleepwalk when they were girls.

Mina searched the house, looking for her friend to guide her back to bed – but the house was empty.

Could she have climbed out the bedroom window? It seemed impossible.

Mina grabbed her coat and searched the garden and street outside. Just as she was about to give up hope, she spotted Lucy in the distance. She was climbing the 199 steps!

Chapter Six

Mina was out of breath and freezing cold as she reached the top of the steps. She spotted Lucy sitting on their usual bench in the graveyard, staring out towards the ruined abbey. Mina pulled her coat around her nightgown and started towards her friend, but something made her stop.

A tall, dark figure was looming over Lucy! Mina could not work out what it was. It looked as big as a man, but it had wings like a crow – or a gigantic bat. Mina cried out in fear. As she did, the creature vanished.

Mina rushed to her friend. Lucy was sitting as still as a statue. She stared straight ahead as though in a trance.

As Mina touched Lucy's arm, she realised her friend was as cold as ice. Gently, Mina guided Lucy away from the graveyard, carefully back down the steps and back into the warmth of the house.

***

'I'm afraid I don't remember a thing,' said Lucy, sipping a hot mug of cocoa the following morning.

'I went to bed and the next thing I know I'm in a chair by the fire in my aunt's sitting room.'

Mina did not mention the strange creature she had seen with Lucy. She did not want to frighten her friend.

'I did have the strangest dream, though,' Lucy said. 'I dreamt that a large bat was flapping against my bedroom window! How peculiar!' Lucy laughed. Mina tried to smile as a shiver shot down her back.

Lucy's aunt stepped into the living room with the morning's letters. 'There is one here for you,

Mina,' she said. 'All the way from Budapest!'

Mina's heart jumped for joy. It must be Jonathan telling her he was on his way home! But as Mina took the letter from Lucy's aunt, she realised it was not Jonathan's handwriting on the envelope.

Budapest General Hospital
Hungary

Dear Miss Murray,

Your fiancé, Mr Harker, is currently at the Budapest General Hospital. He arrived two days ago in some distress and has been asking for you. I think he will feel much better if you are able to visit him here and take him home to England with you.

With warmest wishes,
Sister Florence

Mina gasped, then read the letter aloud to her friend.

'Of course you must go to Jonathan!' said Lucy.

'But what about you?' said Mina. 'You still look terribly pale, and we are meant to be going back to

London today. Are you sure you can make the journey alone?'

Lucy insisted. 'I just feel a little weak,' she said, patting her friend's hand. 'I am sure that after a good rest and some food I will be fine.'

With Lucy's blessing, Mina began to make plans for her journey to Hungary.

Chapter Seven

Mina paused outside the door to Jonathan's hospital ward. The journey to Budapest had taken a day's travel and Mina was exhausted. She took a deep breath and stepped inside. Jonathan was sitting up in his bed, staring at the sun streaming in from the open window.

For a moment he did not see her, then he turned. Mina was shocked at what she saw.

Jonathan's handsome face was thin and pale. There were large dark circles under his eyes and grey in his hair.

'My dearest!' he said in a thin voice, holding out a bony hand. 'I am sorry for how I look. I hope I have not shocked you.'

Mina took Jonathan's hand and sat beside him. 'Of course not,' Mina lied. She tried to hold back her tears. The sight of her fiancé looking so weak and pale was almost as upsetting as seeing Lucy and that creature in the graveyard together.

'What happened?' asked Mina, gently.

Jonathan lifted his arm and pointed to a leather-bound book on his nightstand. Mina picked it up and flicked through the pages. It was a journal crammed with writing and drawings.

'Do not read it,' Jonathan said. 'Inside is everything I witnessed and dreamt about at Count Dracula's castle, and how I escaped from it.'

'Escaped?' Mina said with alarm. 'Why did you need to escape Count Dracula's castle?'

Jonathan's eyes widened. 'That man is not of this world,' he said, his voice trembling a little. 'I fear that if he makes his way to England, terrible things will happen.'

'What sort of things?' asked Mina.

Jonathan shook his head. 'I don't know for sure, but I know that I need your help,' he said. 'Take my journal and keep it safe. We may need it in the future. For now, all I need is for you to be with me, to help me get better and return to England.'

Mina took the journal and wrapped it in the scarf she was wearing. 'There,' she said. 'Now you can forget all about it and concentrate on getting better.'

Chapter Eight

Dr Seward stared at the young man sitting opposite him across his desk. He had heard the man's name before, of course, but had never met him in person. It was Arthur Holmwood, the man his beloved Lucy had decided to marry instead of him.

'What can I do for you, Mr Holmwood?' Dr Seward asked.

Arthur shifted in his seat, feeling just as uncomfortable as

Dr Seward. He was there to ask a favour of the man who loved his fiancée as much as he did.

Arthur cleared his throat. 'I have come to talk about Lucy,' he said at last. Dr Seward raised his eyebrows. 'You see, she is terribly unwell. I have been to my own doctor and he does not know what is wrong with her. Lucy always spoke so well of you. I have come to ask for your help.'

'Lucy is unwell?' Dr Seward said, concern raising in his voice.

Arthur nodded. 'She returned from a holiday in Whitby looking pale and weak. Each night that passes, she seems to fade more and more. Please, Dr Seward,' Arthur said. 'I beg of you to come and see her.'

***

In just one short hour, Dr Seward was at Lucy's bedside. The healthy young woman he once knew had transformed completely. She was thin and pale, and her eyes scanned the room as though searching for something. Dr Seward had to calm his trembling hands to examine her.

'What do you think, doctor?' asked Arthur. 'What can we do to help her?'

Dr Seward took out his stethoscope to listen to Lucy's heart. As he loosened the scarf around her neck, he noticed two small marks. 'What are these?' he asked.

Arthur looked over the doctor's shoulder. 'We think she may have been bitten by some kind of insect in Whitby,' Arthur replied. 'She and her friend Mina were very fond of walking.'

Dr Seward continued his examination, then beckoned Arthur over to the far corner of Lucy's bedroom.

'Mr Holmwood,' he began in a hushed voice so that Lucy could not hear them. 'Lucy is showing all the symptoms of blood loss.'

Arthur stepped back, amazed. 'Blood loss?' he said. 'How?'

'That is just it,' Dr Seward replied. 'There is no sign that Lucy has been injured in any way – apart from the tiny marks on her neck.'

Arthur glanced at Lucy's bed. She had fallen into a fitful sleep. 'What can we do?' he asked.

Dr Seward put on his coat and put his equipment back into his bag. 'I am going to send a telegram this evening to a friend of mine in Amsterdam,' Dr Seward said. 'If he can, he should be with us by this time tomorrow. He has experience of this ...' the doctor hesitated. '... this sort of thing.'

'Thank you, Dr Seward,' said Arthur. 'Is there anything I can do while we wait?'

Dr Seward looked around Lucy's room. 'You can sit in that chair – and don't let her out of your sight.'

telegram

A telegram is a short message that is sent by electric signals between two electrical stations and then printed out onto paper.

Chapter Nine

Abraham Van Helsing arrived at Lucy's house in London the following evening. He came straight from the ship that had brought him from Amsterdam. His carriage had stopped briefly at Dr Seward's office to pick him up.

Now Arthur and Dr Seward watched nervously as Van Helsing examined Lucy. He muttered occasionally, stroking his white beard and writing in a battered notebook.

'She seems a little better this morning,' Arthur said as Lucy dozed. 'Her skin seems brighter.'

'Hmmm,' said Van Helsing. 'And you say you stayed with her all night long?'

'Yes, sir,' Arthur said. 'I sat in that chair over there. It wasn't very comfortable, so I did not sleep a wink.'

Van Helsing nodded and looked from Lucy to the large window next to her bed. He tapped the glass twice with the end of his pen. 'And did anything happen in the night that was … out of the ordinary?' he asked.

Arthur thought for a moment. 'Well, at one point there was something outside the window. It looked like a large black bird – although at that time of the night it was more likely to have been a bat.'

Van Helsing spun around from his spot at Lucy's window and crossed the room in a flash.

‘A bat?’ he repeated loudly. ‘Are you sure it was a bat?’

Arthur looked at Dr Seward in alarm, then back at Van Helsing. ‘I think so,’ he said. ‘It flapped and scratched at the window as though trying to get in. As I drew the curtains it flew away.’

Van Helsing began to pace the room, stopping to flip through the notes in his book. 'It can't be … It can't be …' he muttered to himself.

'Abraham,' Dr Seward said at last. 'If you have any idea what might be wrong with Miss Westenra, or how we can help her, I beg you to tell us.'

Van Helsing nodded and began to speak to Dr Seward and Arthur in a hushed tone. 'Miss Westenra is displaying all the symptoms of something called vampirism,' he explained. 'I have come across it only once before, on a terrifying trip to Romania.'

'But Lucy has been nowhere near Romania!' Arthur insisted. 'And what is vampirism? Is it some sort of disease? Can it be treated?'

'No, it is not a disease, but it can be treated ... I hope,' Van Helsing said. 'I have never attempted it before.'

'But what is it?' asked Dr Seward. 'I knew as soon as I saw the marks on Lucy's neck that it was not normal – which is why I asked you to come.'

Van Helsing took a deep breath. 'There is a man who has lived for over a hundred years and still looks young. It is said he stays young by drinking the blood of those younger than himself.'

Arthur stepped back in horror. 'It can't be true,' he said.

'That is what I thought at first,' Van Helsing said. 'Until I saw the victims myself. They displayed all the same symptoms as Miss Westenra.'

'Arthur?' Lucy called out as she woke. 'Is that you?'

Chapter Ten

Arthur, Dr Seward and Van Helsing decided not to tell Lucy what Van Helsing had discovered. They were concerned the shock of the news might make her worse. Instead, Van Helsing brought strange, strong-smelling flowers to Lucy's room and placed them around her bed and by the window.

'Garlic,' he said to Dr Seward as they were leaving. 'Vampires – those who

practise vampirism – are repelled by the smell. They won't come near her with these in the room.'

Dr Seward did not understand. 'But, if Lucy has already been bitten by a vampire, how will it help?'

'Because vampires come back to the same victim night after

night, until the victim turns into a vampire too.'

Arthur went pale. 'L-Lucy could turn into one of those horrible creatures?' he said.

Van Helsing nodded. 'If the vampire visits her one last time, I am afraid so. The garlic should protect her this evening. In the meantime, we must come up with a plan to find the creature.'

***

That evening, while Lucy slept at her home, the three gentlemen sat in Dr Seward's office to discuss what to do next. Van Helsing's notebook was filled with research on terrible and fearsome creatures he had studied.

'Vampires only come out at night,' he said. 'They have the ability to turn into bats, so when you said a bat had appeared at Miss Westenra's window, I knew just what we were dealing with.'

'Is there any way of getting rid of them?' asked Dr Seward.

'Yes,' replied Van Helsing. 'But it is very dangerous. We must face the vampire ourselves and force it into sunlight. Sunlight turns a vampire into dust.'

'Then that is what we must do,' said Arthur, bravely. 'But first we must go back to Lucy's house. I feel uneasy leaving her alone now that we know what we're up against.'

***

It was dark as Arthur, Dr Seward and Van Helsing approached Lucy's house on a smart London street. Strangely, none of the tall iron streetlamps had been lit, which made the street seem gloomier than usual. As they approached the door, Lucy's housemaid was climbing the steps from the basement with a big bag of rubbish in her hand.

'Oh, 'ello, Mr 'olmwood,' the housemaid said. 'Are you here to see Lucy? I 'ope you 'aven't brought any more of those flowers with you – they stank poor Lucy's room out! I've binned them and opened the windows to get rid of the smell.'

'No!' shouted Van Helsing. He burst through Lucy's front door, closely followed by Arthur and Dr Seward.

They reached Lucy's bedroom in time to see a large, black-winged creature swoop out of her window.

'Lucy!' cried Arthur, running to her side.

Lucy's eyes flickered open. Instead of their usual deep blue colour, they were a burning red. 'Speak to me, Lucy!' Arthur begged. But Lucy's head fell back onto the pillow. Dr Seward picked up her wrist and felt for a pulse.

'We are too late,' he said with a sob. 'Lucy has died.'

Chapter Eleven

Jonathan and Mina walked arm in arm towards Highgate Cemetery. It had been weeks since Mina had found Jonathan in Budapest, and each day he had gotten stronger and stronger. Only when they arrived back in London did Mina learn that her best friend Lucy had died. She was devastated and blamed herself. She had seen that Lucy was unwell

when she left for Budapest, and she could not help wondering if there was something she could have done to help her friend before she went.

Mina clutched a bunch of Lucy's favourite flowers close to her as she knelt and laid them on Lucy's grave. 'I will miss her so much,' sniffed Mina, tearfully. 'The strange thing is no one will tell me what happened to her.'

Jonathan held Mina's arm as they turned to walk away.

'Oi! Watch out, you two!' cried a young boy, running between the gravestones with his friends. 'You don't want the Bloofer Lady to get you!'

'Whatever do you mean, young man?' Jonathan asked.

'The Bloofer Lady! She's been roaming around the graveyard at night with bright red eyes! You wouldn't catch me hanging about here!' And with that, the little boy and his friends ran off.

***

When Jonathan and Mina returned to Mina's house, they found a letter from Arthur Holmwood asking them to meet him at Dr Seward's office that afternoon.

'How strange,' said Mina.

'I wonder what Dr Seward and Arthur want to see *me* about. Especially *together*! I thought they would be enemies. They both proposed to Lucy, you know, but she chose Arthur.'

'Perhaps I should come with you' said Jonathan.

A few hours later, they were sitting in Dr Seward's comfortable

office with him, Arthur and an older gentleman who was introduced as Dr Van Helsing. Once Mina was settled, they told her everything that had happened to Lucy.

'A … a creature called a vampire killed Lucy?' Mina said, breathlessly. She could not quite believe it.

Van Helsing nodded.

'Can you remember anything

about your time in Whitby that seemed strange to you?' he asked.

Mina thought for a moment. She was shaken after hearing all the terrible things that had happened to her friend. She took Jonathan's hand and saw that he had turned pale too.

'Lucy walked in her sleep,' Mina remembered. 'It was the first time she had done it since we were young girls. I followed her all the way to the graveyard by the ruined abbey. There was someone or something with her. It was tall and shrouded in black. I thought it was a person, but they had wings. I know it sounds silly …'

'Not silly to us,' Van Helsing said.

'Then there was the shipwreck, of course,' Mina continued. 'I was told all that survived was a box. A long, thin box, almost the shape of a–'

'Coffin,' Jonathan interrupted. He took a deep, shaky breath. His eyes were wide with fear. 'Gentlemen, I think I know who the vampire may be.'

Chapter Twelve

Mina fetched Jonathan's journal and he began to tell Dr Seward, Van Helsing and Arthur everything that had happened at Castle Dracula.

'When I found the coffin below the count's bedroom, I was so terrified that I left,' he concluded.

'You had a lucky escape,' Van Helsing said. 'The cross the young maid gave you almost certainly saved your life. Like garlic, vampires hate crosses and can't go near them.'

'There is one thing troubling me,' said Mina at last. 'Although I feel foolish saying it out loud.'

Dr Seward let out a nervous laugh. 'A few short weeks ago, I would not have believed what I have experienced. But now, nothing you say will sound foolish to me.'

'When we went to visit Lucy's grave,' Mina began, 'some children warned us about a "Bloofer Lady" who roams the graveyard at night. A Bloofer Lady is a beautiful sort

foolish
Acting silly or having bad judgement in a situation.

of ghost, I think. With red eyes.'

Van Helsing and Dr Seward exchanged glances. 'Oh, no!' said Dr Seward. 'It's Lucy.'

The group looked from one to another, shellshocked.

Arthur rose from his seat angrily. 'No! No! I won't have it,' he shouted. 'My Lucy is not one of those creatures!'

But the mournful silence that followed spoke even more loudly than Arthur's words.

'I'm afraid we have work to do before we can begin our search for Count Dracula,' said Van Helsing with a grim look on his face. 'We must help to end Miss Westenra's suffering.'

***

Just before dawn, Dr Seward, Van Helsing and Arthur made their way, slowly and silently, to Highgate Cemetery. Arthur hoped with all his heart that they would not find Lucy wandering the grounds. However, as they reached the part of the cemetery where Lucy's grave was, they saw a shadowy figure dressed in white.

'Oh no,' Arthur cried, tears filling his eyes. 'It *is* Lucy.' The three men crouched down behind a large tombstone.

'It is as I feared,' said Van Helsing. 'She has become one of the undead, doomed to walk the earth at night.'

'How can we help her?' asked Dr Seward as he comforted Arthur with an embrace.

Van Helsing looked at the sky.

Whisps of daylight were starting to form. 'The sun will soon rise. If we can keep Miss Westenra from returning to her grave, the sun's light will remove the vampirism.'

Van Helsing reached into his pocket and handed Arthur and Dr Seward small wooden crosses to wear around their necks, and a handful of garlic flowers to stuff into their pockets.

‘These should protect you in case Miss Westenra tries to bite you,’ he said.

Arthur shook his head in disbelief. ‘Lucy would never …’

‘But *that* is not Lucy anymore,’ Dr Seward said, kindly. ‘We must banish that creature from Lucy’s body before any further harm is done.’

Arthur nodded, and after a silent count of three, the men stood up to face the figure. She turned and smiled at them with her fanged mouth. Slowly, she began to walk towards them.

Arthur tried hard to keep calm. 'That's it, Lucy, my dear,' he said, softly. 'Come to me.'

The figure stopped and looked at the other men, then towards the sunlight that had started to fill the sky. She made a rush towards her grave, but Van Helsing and Dr Seward blocked her path and held her back. It was then that Arthur saw her try to bite Van Helsing's neck, but Van Helsing held up his cross just in time.

The creature was far stronger than Lucy had been when she was alive. Arthur could see that she was close to breaking free from Van Helsing and Dr Seward's grasp. He rushed forwards and placed his hands on Lucy's shoulders. As more and more sunlight filled the cemetery, the creature inside Lucy's body began to cry out. In a matter of moments, she had turned to dust.

Chapter Thirteen

Mina and Jonathan silently poured tea for the three unhappy men. They were tired, and their faces were stony from the upsetting events that had taken place just a few hours earlier.

'You were very brave,' Mina said at last, placing a hand over Arthur's.

'I only had the strength to do it because I knew that creature wasn't really Lucy,' said Arthur.

'And I,' added Dr Seward. 'As you all know, I was once very much in love with Lucy too. But that was not the girl I loved.'

Arthur and Dr Seward exchanged a sad smile.

'What happened to poor Miss Westenra is only the beginning,' said Van Helsing. 'If we do not find the count, I predict there will be more people who fall under his spell. We must find him, and we must destroy him.'

Jonathan stood up from the table they sat around and walked to his desk. He returned with a

small bundle of letters.

'I know where we will find him,' Jonathan said. 'These are the papers I took with me to Romania. They are the details of the house Count Dracula was to buy in London. I made copies before I handed them back to my firm. Somehow I felt as though I needed to know where he was if he ever made it to England.'

Van Helsing drew the pile towards him. 'Carfax House,' he read aloud. 'Is that far?'

'It is close to my office,' replied

Dr Seward. 'I think we should investigate this evening.'

'Then I will come too,' replied Jonathan. 'I know the count's ways. I may be of help.'

As the gentlemen left to prepare for the coming evening, Mina rested her head on Jonathan's shoulder. 'I understand why you volunteered to go with them,' she began, 'but I feel so scared when I am away from you. So many terrible things have happened. Promise me you will stay safe.'

'Don't worry. All will be well,' replied Jonathan.

***

Carfax House was a large stone building set down a deserted road. It had been empty for many years – forgotten by everyone but the person who was desperate to sell it. The house was cold and damp. Its small windows let in little daylight. The only selling point was its large basement, perfect for storage. Jonathan understood why Count Dracula had chosen the place as his English home.

In the early hours of the morning, the four men gathered

in a dark alleyway opposite Carfax house. Jonathan had brought the room plans from his pile of papers to use as a map once they were able to get inside.

'We all know what we must do,' said Van Helsing, once again passing wooden crosses to Dr Seward, Arthur and Jonathan. They nodded in return. 'Vampires are strong, and this one in particular will have far more strength than Miss Westenra,' Van Helsing warned

them. 'It will take all of us to overpower him and force him into the daylight.'

'We will need to stay together,' added Jonathan. 'When I stayed with the count at his castle, he would appear and disappear as if from nowhere. I believe he uses his power to confuse those around him.'

Van Helsing agreed. 'If we are all ready, let us begin.'

Jonathan checked the room plan before placing it in the inside pocket of his jacket. There was a small window to the side of the house that could easily be opened, allowing them to crawl inside.

'For Lucy,' said Arthur, placing his hand on Dr Seward's shoulder before they climbed inside.

'For Lucy,' Dr Seward replied.

Chapter Fourteen

'I am sorry, gentlemen,' said Jonathan as he led Dr Seward, Arthur and Van Helsing back through the streets of London, away from Carfax House.

'It is not your fault, Mr Harker,' said Van Helsing. 'None of us were to know Count Dracula would not be inside the house. But at least we know he has been there.'

Dr Seward shuddered at the thought of the coffin in the

basement of Carfax House. The terror he had felt when Van Helsing had lifted off the lid.

'With all those large rooms, why does the creature choose to sleep in a coffin? In a basement?' he said.

'They like the dark. The gloom. It keeps them safe,' replied Van Helsing. 'The more I learn about vampires, the more terrifying they become.'

'We shall try again,' said Arthur, determined.

Jonathan said goodbye to the men and headed to Mina's house. Although it was still dark, he wanted to tell her everything that had happened, and to reassure her that he was safe. However, as he approached Mina's door, he felt a sudden uneasiness. It was a feeling he had last felt during his time at Castle Dracula. Without knocking, he burst into Mina's home and sprinted to her bedroom. He was just in time to see the terrible black wings of a bat-like creature escape through the window.

'Mina!' Jonathan cried. 'Mina! No!'

‘J-Jonathan?’ Mina said, breathlessly. ‘It is all right.’

Jonathan helped Mina to sit up in her bed. ‘What happened?’ he asked.

‘It was awful. My maid must have opened a window during the night because when I woke, he was standing over me!’ She threw herself into Jonathan’s arms. ‘But I remembered Dr Van Helsing’s advice. Just as the count tried to bite me, I reached for my silver cross and it worked! He jumped back as though it were a poisonous snake. That was the moment you came in.’

Jonathan held Mina tightly. He trembled at the thought of what could have happened to his beloved fiancée. As he looked down at Mina, his stomach lurched. There was a small mark on her neck. Not a bite, more like a bruise.

'We should take you to Dr Seward's office,' Jonathan said. 'He and Van Helsing should check you over – just in case.'

***

Van Helsing lowered his magnifying glass from Mina's neck, as Dr

Seward, Arthur and Jonathan looked on. He checked his notebook, sighed and paced the room.

'Well?' asked Jonathan, impatiently. 'What do you think? Is it just a bruise or something more?'

'If I am correct,' Van Helsing said, 'the mark is a connection between Count Dracula and Mina.'

'What?' cried Mina, taking Jonathan's hand.

'When the count realised he could not make you one of his victims with a bite, he placed a mark on you instead. But it is not

all bad news,' Van Helsing said. 'The mark provides a connection between you and the count – which means we will know where he is at all times. All you have to do, Mina, is concentrate and make the connection.'

'No!' said Jonathan, forcefully,

standing up. 'I will not place Mina in such danger. We will have to think of another way.'

Silence, like the quiet before a storm, settled in the doctor's office. Nothing but the crackle from the fireplace could be heard. After a moment, Mina slowly stood up and placed a gentle hand on Jonathan's arm.

'My dear, you know that Lucy was my best friend,' she began, softly. 'I have never forgiven myself for leaving her when she was ill. Now she is gone, perhaps this is a way I can help her at last.

By helping to destroy the creature that killed her.'

Jonathan frowned and turned away.

'You are very brave, my dear,' said Dr Seward, tears forming in his eyes.

'Lucy loved you very much, too, Mina,' said Arthur.

Mina looked at Jonathan. He softened and sighed. 'Very well,' he said.

CHAPTER FIFTEEN

Mina sat by the fire in Dr Seward's office, her feet placed on a footrest. Her eyes were closed as she breathed in and out slowly.

'Concentrate, Miss Murray,' said Van Helsing, softly. 'Focus on your mind's eye. Tell us, what can you see? What can you hear?'

Mina shifted in her seat. Her thoughts swam in and out of focus. Then, suddenly, she heard a sound that could not possibly be from the doctor's office. 'I … I hear water,' she said. 'No, waves. Lapping against the side of a boat.'

'What can you see?' asked Van Helsing.

'Sails … A large boat … A ship,' she continued.

Van Helsing looked in alarm at the men in his office. If Count Dracula was on a ship it meant that he had not only left Carfax House but London as well.

'Where is the ship heading?' asked Van Helsing.

'Transylvania,' Mina said, after a moment. She opened her eyes. 'He's escaping!' she cried. 'The coward is running away! We have to stop him! And before any of you try to argue, I am coming too. I can tell you where he is at all times. I won't let Lucy down again.'

Dr Seward, Arthur, Jonathan and Van Helsing were stunned into silence. Then they began to forge a plan.

***

Count Dracula always travelled by ship. It was the only method of transport that could easily house his coffin over such a long distance. However, Arthur knew of a far quicker way to get to Romania: by train.

By that afternoon, the five travellers had boarded the famous

Orient Express that would take them across Eastern Europe to Dracula's home country.

As they travelled aboard the luxurious train, Mina tried to make a connection with Count Dracula again. 'There is nothing but darkness,' she said, as the train rumbled onwards.

'It is daytime,' Jonathan said, looking out the window at the same rolling hills he had passed on his first journey to Romania. 'He will be hiding in his foul coffin until dusk.'

As night fell, Mina was relieved

to tell the gentlemen that she could still hear water and flapping sails when she made the connection. Count Dracula had not reached Romania yet, but the five travellers were about to enter the station in Bucharest. From there they would travel to Transylvania by carriage.

As they gathered their luggage, Mina suddenly gasped. 'He knows!' she said, looking fearfully at Jonathan. 'The connection we share must work both ways. I can see where Count Dracula is – but he can see through my eyes, too.'

Van Helsing threw the rest of the bags onto the carriage.

'Then we have no time to lose,' he said. 'The count will try to outsmart us. We must be ready for him.'

Chapter Sixteen

Once more, Jonathan Harker stood staring up at the looming towers of Castle Dracula. Although it was daytime, the castle seemed to be permanently gloomy. The wind whistled through the stone courtyard, and Jonathan felt that same sense of dread. However, this time he was accompanied by Dr Seward, Arthur Holmwood, Abraham Van Helsing, and his fiancée, Mina.

'The count will have ordered a carriage to pick up his coffin from the port as soon as the ship docked,' said Van Helsing. 'We must tackle it as soon as it arrives at the castle and expose Count Dracula to sunlight – turning him to dust.'

‘Arthur, Jonathan and I will wait on the road,’ said Dr Seward. ‘We will sound the alarm as soon as we hear horses.’

With a quick kiss for Mina, Jonathan joined Dr Seward and Arthur. Mina and Van Helsing began to pace through the courtyard and into the castle gardens.

‘The country is so beautiful,’ Mina said as she looked over Count Dracula’s land.

‘You would not think it was hiding something so dark,’ Van Helsing agreed.

Hours passed and the afternoon

sunlight was starting to weaken.

'He should have been here by now,' Van Helsing said with a sigh. 'Whatever happens, we do not want to be here when the sun sets.'

'What is that?' Mina asked, looking down across the fields to a small, moving dot in the distance.

Van Helsing pulled a pair of binoculars out of his bag. He gasped. 'It is him!' he said. 'It looks like he has hired farm workers to pull him across the fields in a cart.'

'He knew we would be waiting for him on the road!' said Mina.

'Quickly!' said Van Helsing. 'We

don't have much time before the sun sets!'

Mina and Van Helsing ran towards the cart, shouting the names of their companions as they went. 'JONATHAN! ARTHUR!' Mina cried, trying to keep up with Van Helsing.

They reached the cart out of breath. 'The … the … coffin … We … need … to …' Van Helsing gasped. 'We … must … destroy … it!'

The two farm workers who had been pulling the cart looked at each other, confused. 'We've got strict instructions to take it to the castle,' said one.

'We won't get paid if we don't,' said the other.

'Please!' pleaded Mina. 'We don't have time to argue!' She glanced at the setting sun with panic.

'Will this do?' said a voice. Mina and Van Helsing spun around to see Arthur, closely followed by Dr Seward and Jonathan. Arthur held out a pouch of coins. The farm workers dropped the cart and pocketed the coins.

'It's all yours!' they said as they ran away across the fields.

'Quickly!' cried Van Helsing as he and Jonathan climbed onto the cart. 'There isn't much daylight left!' Jonathan ripped off the lid of the coffin to reveal Count Dracula.

His arms were crossed over his chest, his skin as pale as before. But somehow he looked younger than Jonathan remembered. His hair was now black instead of white. Drinking Lucy's blood had made him look younger.

At that moment, the count's eyes popped open. They flashed with anger as he looked from face to face. 'Now!' Van Helsing cried, and the men reached inside the coffin and pulled out the vampire. Count Dracula fought against them, but

as each of the men's crosses swung from their necks, Count Dracula recoiled in horror.

The last rays of sunlight fell against Count Dracula's skin

and he cried out in terror. He turned into dust in the men's arms and just like that, he was gone.

EPILOGUE

My dear Abraham,

I am writing to you to let you know how we are all getting along. It has been a year since those dreadful moments we shared, and I am pleased to tell you that life is good for our little band of heroes. Jonathan and Mina are married. The mark on Mina's neck vanished a few days after they returned to England. Arthur visits Lucy's grave each week, although I believe he is starting to feel a little happier as each day passes.

As for me, I have written a faithful account of everything that happened. I keep it in a locked drawer in my desk – hidden away until someone needs to read it. But I pray that it will never be needed.

Your friend,
Doctor Seward

AUTHOR BIOGRAPHY

BRAM STOKER

Bram (Abraham) Stoker was born in Dublin in 1847. During his time as a theatre critic for the *Dublin Evening Mail*, he met the newspaper's co-owner, Sheridan Le Fanu. Le Fanu wrote gothic stories and inspired Stoker to do the same. The idea for *Dracula* came after a trip to the coastal town of Whitby, England. It has since become one of the most well-known works in English literature.